Things that Happened

Things that Happened

Butterfly Kisses

Things that Happened

Copyright © 2019 by Butterfly Kisses. All rights reserved.

No part of this publication may be reproduced, stored in a retrieval system or transmitted in any way by any means, electronic, mechanical, photocopy, recording or otherwise without the prior permission of the author except as provided by USA copyright law.

This novel is a work of fiction. Names, descriptions, entities, and incidents included in the story are products of the author's imagination. Any resemblance to actual persons, events, and entities is entirely coincidental.

The opinions expressed by the author are not necessarily those of URLink Print and Media.

1603 Capitol Ave., Suite 310 Cheyenne, Wyoming USA 82001
1-888-980-6523 | admin@urlinkpublishing.com

URLink Print and Media is committed to excellence in the publishing industry.

Book design copyright © 2019 by URLink Print and Media. All rights reserved.

Published in the United States of America

ISBN 978-1-64367-346-2 (Paperback)
ISBN 978-1-64367-345-5 (Digital)

10.04.19

CONTENTS

Chapter 1:   People or not Different..9
Chapter 2:   The family..11
Chapter 3:   The Mean One..13
Chapter 4:   The Man. Rated. R. 15
Chapter 5:   The woman's man..r..in 2001 18
Chapter 6:   True Story 23
Chapter 7:   The House, Horror 25
Chapter 8:   Silent, Rater, r,...29
Chapter 9:   The Family...33
Chapter 10: The horror within 35
Chapter 11: Turkey Terror.rated.r...38
Chapter 12: The love he have for her 41
Chapter 13: Crew 46
Chapter 14: The Good Twin and the Bad Twin 51
Chapter 15: The Story of All People 54
Chapter 16: The Long Love..57
Chapter 17: The Lonely One..60
Chapter 18: All the Children in the World..................................63
Chapter 19: Title the Children Story 65
Chapter 20: The Writer 68

Hazel that she couldn't have no more babies that her in side was messed up. But you know catherine and steve go to church they believe in the lord, god and always will and the lord been blessing catherine and husband steve. Now that's another thing hazel hate on catherine about and that's bad because catherine know that our lord, god love all us just the same he don't love no one different than the other hazel go with catherines husband steve's brother jon and its like hazel have some race going on like she have to run and beat catherine but catherine don't feel like that she is the kind of person that want to help family and other people if she can. Catherine don't think she is better than her family and no one at all she try her best to love everybody no matter who they is. That's why she stay to her self to keep down problems so there wont be no problem but you see everyone in gods world be hating on one another and god don't want us to feel that way about each other because god made all of us and he love us the same no different. And catherine and her husband steve are down to earth christians they don't try to be no better than no one else but a lot of people will say that one another is play hating and that's not good at all so you know catherine just try to go on some times and act like everything is ok between her and hazel because we people cant get our blessings hating and talking about one another it just don't happen that way. Another thing catherine know is that its all kind of evil out here that do this to people but some times evil live in all hearts because aint none of us perfect theres only one perfect person our lord and savior jesus christ and the sooner we all down on

 Butterfly Kisses

earth realize that the better things would be that's what I think. Well catherine and her husband talks about this and as I said they go own with they life you know that's all we can do cant do no more well catherine and husband are blessed with 2 grown sons and they familys and two birds and one cat and 3 truly real baby dolls. And a good marriage thank god for everything the end. well my name is Butterfly Kisses and I just wrote this true story about me and one of my cousins I do love my family I just hope that this help other 19th chapter author Butterfly Kisses may 2 2015 11.00 am. Title the bad blood between two. Here is 41 year old catherine and 42 you old hazel now these two women grew up together and never had a problem with one another not ever. They was real close always they are real life cousin and they was friends as well they hung out and helped each other when they could. And then after they grew up they barely saw one or the other they both started having kids and went they way. What others couldn't understand what couldve happen because hazel helped catherine to fight when they were younger it was real bad how they fail out like they did. Well catherine met a man that was gonna become her husband catherine couldn't understand if hazel was jealous of her life or what. But that's what it seemed like it was real bad but catherine went on with her life she would talk to hazel on her phone but how about every time catherine tried to talk to hazel she was going be hind catherines back talking about her. And it got back to catherine every time well one thing catherine told familys and I hope you enjoy my book and keep the lord, god in your life and relationships and believe in him always well may god, bless all.

Saturday, May 2, 2015

THINGS THAT HAPPEN BY AUTHOR BUTTERFLY KISSES MAY.7.2015 SPARTANBURG S.C 29306 864285.0930, FIRST TIME WRITER HOPE EVERYONE ENJOY MY STORIES BE BLESSED.

Thursday, May 7, 2015 3:30 PM

CHAPTER 1

People or not Different

Tuesday, May 5, 2015
6. 2015 6.31pm

I'm gonna start my story off by saying its a lot of different people in the world well at least people say they are different but the way I see we all need to realize. That we all come from one man now I would say that people are different because of the evil that's in some people but we all know that. theres good and evil in the world we can try and explain the goodness out here which is our lord and savoir jesus christ our lord god and the holy ghost. Its been time for some one to wake up and write story's about these different things because the way things going its not gonna be pretty when it end now don't none of us know when the end but I do know and believe in my heart that it cant end good. With things going the way they are going everyone seem to be against each other no matter who they are. All difrent people killing each other again I say it doesn't matter what color we are I feel that everyone need to pull together even if its pulling together with your family but god says that we all are his

 Butterfly Kisses

kids. He made all of us to get alone not be doing the things we do im not gonna tell a lie but my real family is not tight and they shall be and every body that have family need to pull together we all need to not only pull together but we sniring our nose up at one another stop acting like we are different and better then one another some times we get jobs and a little money and start acting like we are better then people. What we fail to realize is that the perfect person was and still is the perfect one is jesus christ I know and always will know that the things we all have is because of jesus christ if it wasn't for him we wouldn't have nothing we wouldn't even be here alive. That's what we do we get out here and think its all about us but its really all about jesus christ our lord, god. In me and husband Bob's home we talk about the lord all the time and like we also say we don't hate no body I don't care who it is are what color they skin. Because I feel when you living for our lord god you have to live gods way and even our lord knows that it is hard but we can try. No matter who we is or what color we may be my point for me writing this story is because our lord, god open my eyes and even I was amaze of the things I see theres people talking about each other and im not gonna leave my self out because im not perfect but I don't do it all the time. Its just all kinds of bad stuff going on and its bad real bad you know I was getting my nails done and it was a chinese lady that did them and I saw the goodness in this lady she was a good person and I saw that by sitting talking to her. Now that's what im talking about we was talking about our husbands and our kids and it felt great and I know that was only god that made that happen all im saying everyone should try and get alone a lot better than what we do because god love us all the same no different. And don't never forget with god for us who can be against us and don't forget he love all us we belong only to god don't never forget this well this is the end of my story. By Carey I thank god for helping me with these story's and everything and I love the lord, god always don't never ever forget god love all and may god bless all.

CHAPTER 2

The family

Back in florida the year 1998 there was 6 sisters now these sisters was very close but all they children wasn't. The only time this faimly would come together was when someone died and half the time they didn't come together then. They all was against one another either they was talking about one another or they was at each others throats they was a bad, bad, family. And also they was money hungry any time someone came into some money everybody was around asking for money or asking to borrow and would not pay back for nothing in the world. Some of them was running around here on drugs real bad or drinking like its the end people could try to talk to them but it didn't do no good. And people was even dying in the family the family was so bad to it was like they didn't care and you know what was so bad sisters against sisters brothers against brothers cousins against cousin. They all acting like they was jealous of one another some leaving town trying to run from the problem saying they cant stay with them some of the grown kids talking about they own mother. They own kids putting them out doors and they don't have no where to go. Parents running around begging for money because they don't have no where to lay they heads they grandkids treating the grand parents like doo, doo it was bad and still is. Some parents had they children took by dss and cant get them back. These kids growing up without they real parents either they lost them because they was on drugs real bad drinking real bad or didn't stay at home with they kids. And some in the family just didn't want they kids there is people in the world that cant have kids or that's having miscarriages. That want kids but may never have kids this family only care about them selves and nobody else really don't know whats gonna become of this family. But you know it might be two in that family that might try to pull the family together but just don't know if its gonna work. And some of the family be saying that the other family member should do this that but not changing they selves. Where is the family now still doing the same thing not trying to be close and cant leave out sisters lying with each others boyfriends its just bad don't really know what to say about this family but they need jesus very much. And that's where a lot of people in the world mess up they don't have the lord, god in they life all of us need the lord, god. But a lot of people don't never repent of our sins and havent accepted jesus christ as they lord cant nobody do nothing without the lord, god. All I can say is that all people need to wake up and smell the coffee and know that the lord, god is very real and that none of us cant do nothing without god. That's the bottom line because our lord, god says so well the thing im saying is that put all trust in the lord, god please remember we all on earth cant do nothing without him by the way this story is about one half of my family. And my name is Butterfly Kissesand I wrote this short story hope you enjoy it the end.

    Thursday, April 16, 2015 9:21 PM

CHAPTER 3

The Mean One

May 5th 2015 11.25am.
There was 42 year old chassie she was what I will call a mean lady chassie was married and had everything she wanted and husband jim could not understand why she was like this. He always be asking why were she looking mean like she always looked they went to church on sundays and jim and chassie believed very strongly in god. Not only did she look at jim mean she looked at almost everyone like that now you know how people be done went through something bad but every body go through something it was like something was eating chassie up in the inside. She and husband been on trips he bring chassie flowers and gifts something just wasn't right and she knew her husband loved her and would do what ever it was he could for her. But also jim talked to everyone including women and men some times chassie didn't like all the part of him talking to a lot of women either but. I don't think it was all about that when chassie was a little girl something happen to her a man that was a friend of the family kidnapped her he didn't kill her but that scared chassie real bad that's enough to scare even a grown woman and this stuff still was with chassie at her older age and also chassie is

 Butterfly Kisses

spoiled real bad. Her parents and family gave her things she wanted when she was little. She had a lot of stuff. You know chassie and her mom was close but chassies mom is dead and I think chassie miss her so bad some times and chassie and jim lost they two babies together so she have a lot of stuff on her mind which that's understandable. But its no ones fault not even chassies maybe some times she blame her self for things but just don't know how to handle it. Are even sit down to talk about it with her husband maybe she don't think he will understand maybe he will maybe he wont lately chassie has been feeling down real bad with her health and that's been on her mind she's been feeling tied she got this bad cough that keep her woke at night and she feel weak a lot but she try to go on any way and take care of her and husbands home. And lately chassie has her mom on her mind her mom been dead for a year now and chassie be thinking about her babies she have in heaven chassie say its rough but she know our lord, god have her and that with our lord, god everything is gonna be ok. Also mothers day is coming up chassie know she have her grandmother mrs wilma jean burpo. And she cant leave out her mother inlaw and inlaws so she will be ok and chassie has her dad james edwards brannon thank god for everything. Well today chassie still around again thank god and as I said she have family surounding her so everything is gonna be ok well chassie and family and inlaws still in church and feel great the end. Let me introduce my self im Butterfly Kisses and I just wrote this short story but without god I cant do nothing and I thank god first and then my husband Bob and all family well every one out there be blessed and may god bless everyone.

Tuesday, May 5, 2015 11:24 AM

CHAPTER 4

The Man. Rated. R.

Once back in 2000 in brooklyn new york there was a 30year old lizzy. She lived in a house alone and she worked at a night club where she had been working as a bar tender and she was very good at it. Every time a person came to the club they asked for lizzy to fix them a drink. One halloween the club was having a party there was a guy walked up to the bar and said would you make me a drink. Lizzy was putting the glasses inside the bar and she said what would you like and the man said a bloody mary lizzy said coming right up and the man said how much. Then lizzy said this is a party its free. Then the man said you not gonna look at me then lizzy stood up and turned around and looked at the man with a smile and she said whats your name. And he said red she started laughing and said what is that your real name he said yes is something wrong and she said no but. That's a odd name and then red said your name is lizzy she said how do you know he said because every one said you make the best drinks in town. Then he said thanks and walked away later that night. lizzy was getting ready to leave and red was *waiting for her and he said could I walk you home lizzy said yes and they was walking and red said. Im new in town can you show me around town tomorrow night lizzy said yes I will and im off tomorrow. So they arrived at lizzy*

home then red said we here lizzy said thankyou red said my pleasure and then he walked away. Lizzy went in the house and stood at the door for a minute and smiled the next day lizzy was getting ready so that she could show red around town. And the phone ring it was lizzy's best friend from work chaz then chaz said what are you doing lizzy said getting ready to go out with red. Chaz said really then lizzy said don't get no ideals im just showing him around town and then chaz said yea. yea. Details tomorrow bye.then there was a knock at the door lizzy open the door and there was red he looked at lizzy from. Feet to head, she had on red heal shoes white fish net stockings a long red dress red lips makeup very nice and long straight hanging blond hair. Red said you look very beautiful as lizzy looked at red from feet to head his shoes shined black black fully suit. with his white skin and shaved face and cold black hair lizzy said you look very handson your self then red said shall we. Yes we shall then they walked through town as the wind was blowing through lizzy's hair red stared at her and said are you. Hungry lizzy said yes then red said lets go to my home I want to make dinner for you lizzy said I would like that so they went to reds house. As red cooked he gave lizzy some red wine and then red put on some slow music then they sat down to dinner. Then red was looking at lizzy and he got up and motion his hands for her to come to him. Then they started dancing and red turned lizzy around and started kissng her neck then lizzy told red to make love to her. Then red bit her lizzy woke up in her bed then she thought to her self how did I get here she did'nt remember nothing. A few days went by lizzy had not seen red she was disappointed but later that night lizzy was behind the bar and red walked in. he walked up to the bar and said hey my sweet lizzy said im not your sweet I cant believe I made love to you and did'nt see you for a few days just go away. Then red said lizzy look at me im so sorry the work I do it keep me so tied til all I can do is sleep. Lizzy said how do I believe you I don't know if you have another woman or not red said lizzy you was at my home how could you think that im falling in love with one woman and that's you. I aint never felt this way for no one not ever and to prove it will you marry me then lizzy wrapped her arms around red and said you bet I will. Red im so in love with you lizzy said I get off in a little bit im going home with you and lizzy was closing the club. Red took lizzy to his house and they drink wine and again red bit lizzy she woke up at home again then there was a knock at the door. Lizzy open the

Things that Happened

door and it was her friend chaz lizzy said hey what you doing here chaz said details. Lizzy said what are talking about chaz said lizzy im talking about red lizzy said everything is good with me and red. Chaz said when am I gonna meet him lizzy said come by tonight and I will let yall meet, chaz said ok me and tim will come by then chaz hugged lizzy and said see you tonight. And then chaz looked at lizzy's neck and said lizzy whats with the holes in your neck lizzy said its nothing I think something bit me. Chaz said see you tonight later that night chaz and tim got to lizzy's and said hey girl we here where is red lizzy said he will be here. Then a knock was at the door lizzy open the door and said come in im glad to see you. And she hugged and kissed him then she told red this was afriend chazz and her boyfriend tim. Red, shaked his head and said nice to meet you both then chaz grabbed lizzy's hand and whisperd that's why you been busy he very good looking. Then everyone sat down and ate dinner and then lizzy played slow music and everyone danced then chaz looked in the mirror where lizzy and red was. And red had no reflection in the mirror then chaz said o and then she said I just forgot lizzy I have to go and then she said tim lets go. Chaz said it was nice to meet you red but im running late then chaz and tim went out the door tim said whats wrong chaz she said red did'nt have a reflection in the mirror. Then she said tim let me out I cant leave lizzy with him then she went back and said lizzy I need to talk with you where is red. Lizzy said he lef chaz said those marks on your neck they from a vampire red is a vampire lizzy said what are you saying then red appeared and said she telling. You im a vampire lizzy said red no. no you not then chaz said he did'nt cast a reflection in the mirror then red appeared behind chaz and said everything was fine into you open your mouth you should have lef. Now I have to kill you then red bit her and broke her neck lizzy was hollowing red what have you done I loved you red said tell me you don't love me and I will go away forever lizzy said no I still love you then red made chaz disappeared and bit lizzy one last time then she. Became reds queen and they both turned to big bats and flew off they was talking lizzy said I guess this mean I wont have kids red said we will have kids. Then lizzy said how will they come out to play red said I guess they have to come out at night then they both laughed. Then chaz appeared and she was a vampire she said I like my self like this caught a rat and ate him the end.

CHAPTER 5

The woman's man..r.. in 2001

There was 28year old angie she just had moved to alanta georgia to open up her first business a shop that sold on sexy women under wear bras. And other sexy things for women right alone with her co, worker lannya 25year old young woman she met when she first moved to town. One day angie was in the back of the store when a young man walked in lanny said hello welcome to angie's shop im lanny how can I help you. the man said I need to see your manager lanny said she's busy I can help you he said I need to see your manager then lanny said ok. Then lanny said angie there is someone here to see you then angie came up front and said how can I help you then the man took off his sun glasses and said hey angie how have you been. then angie said rick hey how have you been he said good, you looking good, angie you still look the same and then they hugged then lanny cleared her throat then angie said rick this is lanny my co, worker then angie said this is rick. We dated in high school then rick and lanny shook hands and both said nice to meet you then rick said angie youi do eat lunch would you join me for lunch. Then angie

Things that Happened

looked at lanny and lanny said angie go ahead I have the shop then angie said let me get my coat and purse and I will be ready. Then angie and rick lef and then lanny said what a man then angie and rick was laughing and talking about old times when rick said angie I never got over you. Im still in love with you now I don't always do this but if you would have me I would like to see more of you if you not seeing anyone of course angie said im not seeing anyone and yes I would also like to see more of you. then they kissed rick then dropped angie back at work rick walked angie to the door and kissed her and said I will see u tonight angie said ok. as angie walked into the shop lanny said somebody had a good time. Angie said rick is a gentlemen I had a great time he treated me like a queen a few months passed and angie had been seeing rick for about 5 months then one morning angie got up from bed and she was sick on her stomache and dizzy not feeling to good so she called the shop. And told lanny that she was sick and not opening the shop to day that she was going to the doctor then lanny said ok hope you feel better then they hung up one hour later angie was at the doctor and the doctor came in fully checked angie and told her she was two months pregnant. Angie said what o, my god the doctor said congraulations angie said thanks. The doctor said I need to see you back in a month. Angie said ok doctor, that night rick came home and angie said how was your day rick said it was ok im tied then angie said I have something to tell you as tears was in her eyes rick said what is it whats wrong angie said nothing wrong its all good. Angie said in september we will have a baby rick looked at angie and said are you serious angie said I seen the doctor today. Rick got down on one knee and said angie will you marry me angie said yes rick I will i will marry you. Few years later rick went by the shop to take angie to lunch but she had went out to pay a bill lanny told rick that she needed him to lift this box that was in the back room. Rick followed lanny to the back room when they were in the back lanny got close to rick and started rubbing all over him then she started to kiss him then rick said stop. Then lanny said rick no one will know just us then lanny and rick started. kissing lanny took off ricks clothes then rick took off her clothes and they made love. One hour later angie got back and saw lanny behind the counter.

 Butterfly Kisses

and rick was just leaving angie said was we suppose to have lunch he said yes but its time for me to get back to. work then he kissed her and said see you at home then he lef few days later angie was home spending time with her son and the nanny carry was there as well. The bell ring angie open the door it was lanny angie said hey, lanny said hey, angie said come in lanny said I need to talk to you angie said ok and told carry to take her son ricky and put him down for a nap. Carry said yes mam as angie kissed him on his fore head angie said lanny would you like something to drink lanny said no im good. Then angie said whats up lanny said a few months ago when you got back to the shop and rick was leaving angie said yea lanny said me and rick had sex. Angie said what as carry was listening then angie started screaming how could you do this get the hell out of my home don't never come here again. And you are fired lanny said you can't fire me I quit and went out the door and slammed it then angie told carry to watch ricky to she come back. Angie went to ricks job he was a supervisor at a fire department angie walked in and asked rick how could you do it with tears in her eyes rick said. What are you talking about angie said I know you slept with lanny then angie said I want you to come and get your clothes out of my house and never come back and she said you will never see your son again not ever and she lef. everyone in the fire department was looking at rick then rick yelled get back to work all of you later that evening as rick went to lanny's home and knocked on the door hard and yelled lanny I know you in there open this door. Lanny said no go home to your wife rick said you know I cant why did you tell angie, lanny said because you only had sex with me you don't want me. Rick said I can't leave my family lanny said now you don't have a family rick said I will kill you and then he lef, 2years had went by and angie was just getting home from work when carry said mrs angie can I talk to you angie said yes. As she sat down carry said mrs. Angie im not messing in your business but I been knowing lanny and I know her so well that she broke up another marriage and the wife was killed. Angie said what carry said yes mam then carry said lanny temp the men real bad and they really can't help them selves and then carry said I would go and fight for my marriage because lanny have done this before. Then the

Things that Happened

phone ring carry picked up the phone and it was rick and carry said hello and rick said im sorry can I speak to angie. Then carry said mrs. Angie its for you angie got the phone and said hello then rick said im sorry that im calling I just miss our son how is he angie said. He miss you to, rick said can I see him angie said yes come by tomorrow noon rick started crying and said thank you angie said you welcome see you then. Rick said ok thankyou again then they hung up the next day rick arrived and angie open the door rick said hey how are you with roses in his hand he said these are for you. Angie said thankyou come in. rick said thankyou then angie called ricky and said your dad is here ricky ran out and said daddy and rick said there is my boy as he hugged him with tears in his eyes. Then angie said rick I need to talk to you rick said ok whats wrong angie said nothing is wrong we want you to come back home. Rick said what angie said you heard me bring all your stuff home rick grabbed angie and kissed her carry walked in and smiled and said that's good. A few months later angie went to lanny's house and knocked on the door angie said lanny I know you in there. and then the door opened then angie walked in and the door closed and lanny came from behind the door and hit angie real hard in the back of her and angie passed out. Few hours later rick got home and carry said mrs. Angie lef earlier and she aint got home yet so rick said I will go by her work and check on her when rick got in his car cell phone rung and it was lanny she said if you ever want to see angie again you will get over here now.

Rick said if you hurt her I will kill you lanny hung the phone up then rick called the police station and explained what was happening and ask +the police to meet him at 2145 stevens street rick arrived at lanny's and knocked on the door and said im here. Lanny open the door but she said no I will kill her and then detective connie said lanny my name is connie can I come in and talk to you lanny said no and then lanny said rick you suppose to came alone. Then detective connie waved for the officers to go around back and she told lanny I know how you feel and then lanny yelled you don't know how I feel. As connie was talking to lanny the police officer was coming in the back door as lanny was turned facing the front door the officer saw angie on the kitchen floor and blood was coming from her head

 Butterfly Kisses

but she was a live. And then the police waved his hand for her to be quiet and the officer walked up behind lanny and told her to put the knife down. Lanny turned around and was running toward the officer with the knife and the cop shot her. Angie was crying and rick ran to her and said its ok now and then the detective and officer and ambulance was clearing things out and rick said thankyou to all of them 1month later. Angie rick and they son was sitting at home laughing and playing when angie told rick she was pregnant rick grabbed her and said I love you and ricky and our baby on the way. Then lanny was in the crazy house pulling her hair out the end.

    Thursday, February 12, 2015 10:12 AM

CHAPTER 6

True Story

Back in year 1983 there was 16 year old Bob he lived in some apartments with his mom and brothers and sisters now Bob was cool. He always was by him self he was a drinker but was good people. One summer back in 1983 there was 13 year old Iris Thomas. Who came to spend that summer with her aunt elaine. And one morning Iris Thomas was sitting at the kitchen window and she saw Bob walking down back street. And said to her self who is that then aunt elaine came in and asked what are you looking at. Iris Thomas said nothing. The next day Iris Thomas was on the front porch when she saw Bob again but he didn't see her. Then aunt elaine came out on the porch and she saw Bob for the first time and said so you been looking at. That young guy and aunt elaine said why don't you go and say hello but Iris Thomas said no I cant let him see me with these ponytails in my hair. aunt elaine said lets go and fix your hair couple hours later a man came buy to see aunt elaine his name was ricky. aunt elaine said ricky this is my niece Iris Thomas and Iris Thomas this is my friend ricky they both said hello. Then aunt elaine told ricky come here for a minute then she said Iris Thomas like your cousin, ricky said who Bob aunt elaine said yes I think so take her

 Butterfly Kisses

and let her meet him. Then ricky said come and let me take you to the store for your aunt then they lef ricky went up the hill where he saw Bob and his brother. ricky said yall come and take a ride with me. so they drove off, during the ride Bob's brother told him look how that girl looking at you and Bob looked around and saw Iris Thomas looking at him then Iris Thomas put her hand out the window and Bob grabbed her hand. after that the two started dating one month later Bob had to go to job corp and he and Iris Thomas splitted up. Why they were split up. everyone that Iris Thomas met was not like Bobackie had a son in 1988 whom she name franklin lamont reed. After two decades Iris Thomas ran back into Bob again the two got back together only this time they stayed together. after being together 3years they gave birth to they first child together datarius eugene j whom they lost at birth. and almost 2years later they were pregnant with they second child whom they lost in the tube but let me tell you something Bob and Iris Thomas join the church turned they life around and put all trust in god. And there is nothing more important to them then our lord and savior jesus christ also may 1st Iris Thomas lost her mom to lung cancer still she continue always will love our lord in heaven no matter what. because she and fiancee Bob know that during everything that happen the lord always have and always be there for them you know after everything that happen the lord jesus christ has blessed them both. very very well in a way that cant explain and they thank our lord in heaven and never will stop thanking him where are Bob and Iris Thomas today which is jan. 26 2015 well lets just say they are very blessed from the heavenly father Iris Thomas's son frankie is 27 and Bob's son dontaye is 18 frankies married and I have a little grand daughter me and Bob and twin grand sons on the way we are very bless brothers and sisters put trust and faith in our lord and savior jesus christ because he love all us no matter who we is don't never forget our lord god love us and with him for us who can be against us and he say yes who dare say no. god bless you all. by the way im Iris Thomas and husband is Bob and I wrote this short story hope everyone enjoy it again god bless all. by Butterfly Kisses.

    Friday, January 23, 20159:08 AM

CHAPTER 7

The House Horror

Back in california the year 1989 there was a family fighting to get out of. the house. all the family died accept the dad jerome. Then the year 2001 there was a new family that moved into the house there was 30year old Bob. 29 year old pregnant wife judy. 4year old amy next morning judy put amy down for a nap judy was still putting stuff away from they move When she heard a sound and she went to check it out the basement door was cracked open so she closed it. Later that evening Bob arrived home and kissed his wife and asked how was her day judy said good how was. Your day Bob said it was alright then amy ran in and said daddy. daddy Bob said there she is my little angel then they sat down to dinner. When they heard a noise then Bob went and checked it a glass had fell from the cabinet. Bob told judy come and look at this and judy said this morning when I was still unpacking I heard a noise and when I checked it out the basement door was cracked Bob said. I will get someone out here to take a look at it the next morning judy was in the kitchen making breakfast her and amy when judy's water broke. She went into labor Bob got judy to the car and picked amy up locked the house. up and they went to the hospital where. Judy gave birth to a 8pound 5ounce son whom they named danny 8 years passed amy was 12years old and danny is 8. judy

 Butterfly Kisses

was down in the basement doing laundry when she heard danny talking to someone and she knew he was the only one in the kitchen. Amy was in the living room listening to music judy came up stairs and said who are you talking too. Danny said my friend judy said a maginary friend danny said no then he pointed behind her when judy turned around there was a showder figure behind her. then she pulled danny up and yelled and told amy to come on as they ran out of the house judy called Bob from her cell phone that was in her back pocket and she told Bob to get home right away 20minutes later Bob drove up and said whats wrong judy told Bob what had happen and Bob told her that. It was just her imagination running away with her as they was going in the house they neihbor annie called judy and said can I talk to you judy said hey annie whats up. annie said do you know what happen to the family who lived here before you then Bob said judy come on we ready for lunch then judy went in the house. Later that night the kids were in the bed asleep and judy and Bob was laying in bed talking judy said Bob. I know what I saw Bob said this is a old house that when he brought the house there was nothing bad said about this house. Then judy said annie asked me did we know what happen to the people who use to live here Bob said annie is old and you cant listen at to much she say. Then judy and Bob started to kiss as they took off each others clothes and making love later that night there was a loud scream. And Bob and judy ran to the kids room and danny was gone. It was like he disappeared then amy ran in and said whats going on judy said danny is gone amy said what do you mean Bob said its like he dissapeared then they all started calling danny's name there was no answer. Then Bob called the police 20minutes later the police arrived alone with detective canne and partner jose the detective's ask what happen. Bob said our son danny is missing detective canne said when was the last time you saw him then judy said right before bed. Then detective jose said what happen to make you think that danny was missing. Crying judy said we was all sleep and we were woke by a loud scream then detective canne said he went missing from the house. Bob said yes then detective canne told the other police officers to check the house to see if they could find danny. The officers checked the house up and down and danny was'nt no where detetive canne said do yall think he Ran away then Bob said we don't know. Then detective canne said im gonna need yall to come *down to the station in the morning to give a report. Judy had cried so much that her eyes was red then canne said he was so sorry that they was gonna find danny then the detectives lef. The next morning Bob, judy and amy went to the police station detective canne said I have to ask yall something but its just my job. Did anyone of you have anything to do with danny's disappearance they all said no we didn't we want to fine out what happen just as much as you do. Then detective canne said I believe yall then he gave Bob one of his cards and said if you can think of something let me know. Then all said we will thankyou detective then canne said we will be in touch few month's later Bob was at work and amy was in school. And judy was cleaning the house when a knock was at the door it was annie then judy open the door. Then annie said can I talk to you but out side then judy said ok they were sitting on the porch when judy said what's up. Annie said the family that lived here before you and your family the whole family died here accept the dad he still is alive. His name is jerome he stay close to here annie said you need to go see him that maybe he could help you. Save your family judy said annie what are you talking about annie said your home is alive the house is what everybody call this house annie said this house killed that family and now it have your son. Judy said what is jeromes address annie gave judy the address and said go see him judy said thankyou annie and she lef. Judy arrived at jerome's and knocked on the door jerome said who is it judy said jerome white he said who are you she said my name is judy parks and me and my family live at your old house jerome open the door and told judy come in. Jerome said would you like something to drink judy said no thanks then jerome said you and your family have to leave that house judy said the house have my son. And I can't leave, to I get him back judy said can you tell me about the house jerome said in a loud voice that house not only took my family but it killed my family as jerome was crying. judy said im so sorry what happen to your family but please tell me how to stop the house with tears in his eyes jerome said you can't kill that house. As judy was leaving jerome said please get your family away from the house judy lef when she got home she told Bob and amy to get packed we going to a hotel then Bob said what is going on. Then judy said lets go tell you later when they got to the hotel they ate dinner then amy went to bed then judy said Bob the house is alive Bob said what do you mean. Judy said I went*

 Butterfly Kisses

to see the only family member today that survived that house then judy's cell phone ring it was annie. Judy said what's up annie and annie said what is going on at your house judy said what do you mean annie said lights is going on and off and I even hear noise judy said annie we not home we at a hotel. Then annie said please don't come back to that house judy said in a few days we will be back and im gonna destroy. that house then she hung up the phone and Bob looked at her real hard and said I hope you know what you doing and judy said trust me I do. Few days later judy and family went back to the house judy yelled at the house and said give my son back. Then a big showder figure appeared and said noooo, then another showder figure appeared and said you will never get danny back he belong here. Judy said you can't have my son we love him then judy yelled loud danny sweet heart we love you then the big showder grabbed Bob and pulled him through the wall then the other showder grabbed amy. And pulled her through the wall then judy said give me my family then the big showder pushed judy out of the house. Judy was beating on the door annie saw what was happening. And she got on the phone and called jerome and she told jerome you need to come and help judy kill the house he said no I cant im sorry. Then he hung up the phone judy was out side crying then a few minutes later jerome came up. Judy said please help me the house have my family jerome said I can help you kill the house and the only way. Is to blow the house up but your family will survive do you trust me judy looked at jerome with tears in her eyes and said. Yes I trust you then he open his trunk and there was a bomb jerome told judy get way, way, back then jerome throwed the bomb at the house and he ran grabbed judy's hand and they fell on the ground the whole house blowed up. As loud screams came out of the house then there came Bob hugging danny and amy judy was crying as she ran to her family. Then jerome started smiling and annie said thankyou jerome and then jerome looked at judy and judy said thankyou so much jerome said you welcome. As jerome was walking away annie said jerome look as he turned around there was his family alive as his family ran to him he said I thought yall was dead. As they was hugging the police came and it was detective canne he said whats happening here annie said jerome did your job. The detective looked and could'nt believe what he saw as he looked at annie she smiled and then detective canne smiled and shook his head. And got in his car and pulled off the end.

CHAPTER 8

Silent. Rater. r..

Back in 2000 there was 38year old pat and she lived alone in the town of charlotte north carolina. Pat worked all the time she loved her work she was a lawyer took this after her father he was a lawyer before he passed. But pat did have her mom jane and the two was very close it wasn't nothing pat wouldn't do for her mom. One night the two was sitting down having dinner when jane asked pat have she met any one yet. Of course I havent pat said mom when will I ever have time I work all the time jane said my friend anne's son is in town pat said mom no way. Jane said im not saying marry him I just want you to say hello pat said mom you know I love and respect you very much but mom please im not ready to meet no one ok. Jane said ok and then there was a knock at the door jane open the door and standing there was a very attractive young man named ben. from feet to head his. Shoes was shined his dress pants was creast his dress shirt fitted him to the tee his lips was very sexy and nice nose eyes was deep blue eye brows black with cold black and shinie hair. Jane turned around and said pat this is my friend anne's son ben pat got up out of her seat and said hey, hey, im, im, pat and ben said with a smile its nice to meet you my name is ben. Then pat smiled and said

 Butterfly Kisses

its very nice to meet you ben, and he said like wise then jane said ben we was having dinner wont you join us ben looked at pat and said sure I will love to. A few days passed and pat was at her office when a knock at her door and it was a delivery man with flowers. Pat smiled and said whats this the delivery man said could you sign for these pat said sure and then again she said who are these from the man said read your card and he lef. Pat read the card they were from ben and the card said will you have dinner with me I will pick you up at 8.00 then the card said flowers for a flower. Later that night ben knocked on the door and pat open the door and said hey ben and then ben said hey your self and then. Ben said you ready for dinner and pat said yes and then they lef at dinner pat ask ben are you from here. Ben said yes but when I turned 18 I went to the army pat said for real because I cant believe and ben said what do you mean pat said I thought when a person been in the army and then ben said you think something be wrong with them and pat said well yes. Ben said believe it or not ive had my problems pat said if you don't mind me asking what do you mean ben smiled and said. Im 39 years old and when I first got out of the army I couldn't walk pat said what do you mean. Ben pulled up his pants leg and showed pat a scar that looked real bad then pat said im so sorry ben said you don't have to be sorry thanks to the lord god that things wasn't worst ben told pat that his best friend died fighting a battle. Ben said he died right in front of me pat dropped her head and said that's terrible. ben said yea but I believe he went to heaven because he was a good person. And then pat lift her glass and said to your friend and then ben lift his glass and said to my friend. The year 2005 came and pat and ben was still seeing each other pat and ben went to pats mom house and bens mom was there as well. Pat hugged her mom and then hugged bens mom anne and then ben hugged his mom and then hugged pats mom jane. They all was sitting down to dinner when ben said I have something to say everyone looked at him as he got down on his knee tears. Was in both moms eyes as ben pulled out a ring and said pat we been together for 5years and I know you are the one for me will you do me the honor of becoming my wife pat said. Yes with tears in her eyes then she hugged him a few months past before the wedding

Things that Happened

ben was at work and pat was doing they laundry when in bens pocket was a picture and a note. The picture was of a man and the note said ben I will always love you and you know this all the time I spent with you I will never forget it. And you really know how to make a man feel good, pat dropped the note and the picture and started throwing all his stuff out of her house. She was crying later that day ben got home and he said hey how was your day and tried to kiss pat when she said no stop just stop your act. How could you do this I loved you, ben said I don't know what I did and then pat showed him the picture and the note. Pat said you sick, ben said let me explain pat said get the hell out of my house go get out of here and don't never come back. ben lef and then pat went to annes house and said did you know and anne said knew what and pat said that your son was screwing men and then anne dropped her head and then pat yelled answer me and anne said yes I knew but I didn't accept it that's why I let him meet you pat said how dare you and then jane came in and said whats going on and pat said please mom tell me you didn't know and then anne said no she didn't. Then jane said know what and then pat said ben go with men then jane said what, what, then pat ran out and jane looked at anne and said how dare you and your son and then jane was walking off and anne said im so sorry. Jane looked at anne and said you and your son stay away from me and my daughter and then jane said our friend ship is over goodbye anne. Then anne broke down crying jane ran after pat and hugged her and said pat im sorry I didn't know im so sorry. About 6months later pat was out having drinks with a friend and ben walked up to her and said hey pat and she looked up and said what are you doing here and ben said I need to talk to you and pat said no, no,. We don't have nothing to talk about and she got up and ben was blocking her way and she said get out of my way then the guy friend pat was with said the lady asked you to get out of her way and then ben said who is this your new man pat said that's none of your business. Then pat and and her friend man alex was leaving and ben pushed alex down and pat said what the hell you did that for then alex hit ben in his face and ben fell then alex told ben stay away from pat and leave her alone you got that. 1month later pat and alex was drinking wine at pats house and

Butterfly Kisses

then they started kissing and taking each others clothes off and they made love. Out side pats bedroom window there was ben looking in at pat and alex pat got up and went to the kinchen. To get more wine when she heard a loud noise then she ran back to the bedroom and there was ben with a gun. He had hit alex in the head. And knocked him out pat said ben what do you want ben said I want you don't you know this pat said yes ben please don't hurt alex he don't have nothing to do with us. Ben said us and pat said yea im gonna leave with you and we gonna be together do you hear me ben said yes. Pat said ben put the gun down and lets go then ben put the gun down and as pat and ben was leaving alex grabbed the gun and said ben I told you to leave pat alone ben turned around and ran toward alex and fell on the gun and the gun went off. In slow motion pat ran over to them and said alex, alex, are you ok then the police came and pat and alex told them what happen and the ems got there and took alex to the hospital and alex and pat was ok. 2months later pat was in her office and anne came by she said pat can I say something pat dropped her head anne told pat that she knew ben was gay but she didn't want to believe it so she thought if he met a woman and loved her he would get straight but he didn't anne started crying and said iam sorry pat hugged her and said I forgive you mrs anne. Later that day jane pat and alex was sitting there having lunch then pat said mom me and alex getting married then jane dropped her head and pat said mom whats wrong jane looked up and smiled with tears in her eyes and said god answerd my prayer. Then jane hugged both of them and said I love yall the end. silent, suspense.

    Thursday, March 5, 2015 6:23 PM

CHAPTER 9

The Family

Back in florida the year 1998 there was 6 sisters now these sisters was very close but all they children wasn't. The only time this faimly would come together was when someone died and half the time they didn't come together then. They all was against one another either they was talking about one another or they was at each others throats they was a bad, bad, family. And also they was money hungry any time someone came into some money everybody was around asking for money or asking to borrow and would not pay back for nothing in the world. Some of them was running around here on drugs real bad or drinking like its the end people could try to talk to them but it didn't do no good. And people was even dying in the family the family was so bad to it was like they didn't care and you know what was so bad sisters against sisters brothers against brothers cousins against cousin. They all acting like they was jealous of one another some leaving town trying to run from the problem saying they cant stay with them some of the grown kids talking about they own mother. They own kids putting them out doors and they don't have no where to go. Parents running around begging for money because they don't have no where to lay they heads they grandkids

Butterfly Kisses

treating the grand parents like doo, doo it was bad and still is. Some parents had they children took by dss and cant get them back. These kids growing up without they real parents either they lost them because they was on drugs real bad drinking real bad or didn't stay at home with they kids. And some in the family just didn't want they kids there is people in the world that cant have kids or that's having miscarriages. That want kids but may never have kids this family only care about them selfves and nobody else really don't know whats gonna become of this family. But you know it might be two in that family that might try to pull the family together but just don't know if its gonna work. And some of the family be saying that the other family member should do this that but not changing they selves. Where is the family now still doing the same thing not trying to be close and cant leave out sisters lying with each others boyfriends its just bad don't really know what to say about this family but they need jesus very much. And that's where a lot of people in the world mess up they don't have the lord, god in they life all of us need the lord, god. But a lot of people don't never repent of our sins and havent accepted jesus christ as they lord cant nobody do nothing without the lord, god. All I can say is that all people need to wake up and smell the coffee and know that the lord, god is very real and that none of us cant do nothing without god. That's the bottom line because our lord, god says so well the thing im saying is that put all trust in the lord, god please remember we all on earth cant do nothing without him by the way this story is about one half of my family. And my name is Butterfly Kissesand I wrote this short story hope you enjoy it the end.

Thursday, April 16, 2015 9:21 PM

CHAPTER 10

The horror within

There was 12year old cindy cox she was a very nice young girl she got all a s on her report card and everything her parents ask of her it was done. But cindy could see ghost and her mom katie cox believed her but her dad john cox didn't he thought cindy did this to get attention. One weekend cindy and her family went on a vacation to this big hotel it was the biggest hotel in town. Cindy and her family went out to dinner then they came back to the hotel where katie put cindy down for the night while her and john sat down to watch. A movie everything was going good they was sipping on wine laughing and talking when they heard cindy scream. And they ran to cindy's room and asked her what was wrong cindy told her parents that there was a little boy in her room. And then john started to look around her room where he saw nothing and then john told cindy she just doing this for attention but katie said john I believe her. Then john lef out of the room and cindy said why daddy don't believe me and katie said because your dad cant see what you see. Then katie hugged cindy and said its gonna be ok 6years later passed and cindy was having her 18th birthday party. With all her friends and family cindy went to the bathroom and shut the door and a young man

 Butterfly Kisses

appeared to her and he said cindy don't be afraid. And cindy said how do you know my name the young man said cindy I know you because ive been with you all your life she said what do you mean. He said you will know soon and he disappeared then cindy best friend sheila said are you ok cindy open the door and said im fine. Then shiela said well come on then theres a guy out here waiting for the birthday girl and cindy started smiling. Then katie cindy's mom said come here cindy I need to talk to you then cindy hugged her mom and said whats up katie said now you is gonna start dating but don't let them know about your secrets because they might not believe you. Then cindy said ok mom I promise then katie hugged cindy and said go and have a good time. 4years later cindy was 22years old she was a grown woman cindy was a secetary at a big law firm and she was sitten at her desk when a nice looking young man walked in he said hello my name is ryan and she said hello, hello my name is cindy and ryan said can you help me. And cindy said I will try and ryan said im new to the law firm but I don't know where to go cindy said what floor you suppose to go to. And he said 3rd floor and cindy said come I will take you to that floor and ryan said I don't want to run you away. But im new and I want to ask you to lunch cindy said I would love to have lunch with you and dinner and ryan smiled. Then cindy and ryan started dating cindy parents liked ryan and ryan parent's liked cindy one night cindy ryan and they parents was having dinner. When ryan said cindy will you marry me and cindy said you bet I will marry you and ryans parents connie and jim tokel. Jumped up and hugged both of them and said they was very happy they been wanting this because they love cindy. Then cindys mom katie jumped up and hugged both of them and said yall just don't know how happy iam. But john knew what they went through with cindy growing up but he hugged them any way. Then john said cindy can I speak to you cindy said sure dad everyone I will be right back john told cindy I will pay for the wedding but. Ryan and his family cant know your secret cindy said after we married iam gonna tell my new husband whats going on with me. John dropped his head 2months later cindy and ryan was married and they went on they honey moon to califonia. And they was out on the town drinking and having a good time kissing and hugging and laughing when a woman walked up to them and she called them by they names. Then cindy said how do you know our names the woman said cindy you are a special one cindy said what do you mean. Then the lady who name was jean said you will know soon and she lef ryan said cindy are you ok and cindy said yes iam. Later that night back at they hotel cindy and ryan made love and then they fell asleep later over in the morning cindy heard her name called she woke up and said what. Ryan was still sleep cindy got up and followed a light and when she got down the hall there was jean cindy said how did you get in here jean said im a ghost cindy said what and jean said yes iam. Then cindy said what do you want then jean said cindy the first ghost you saw when you was 12 he was ryan your husband cindy started laughing and jean said its true and cindy said yes right and cindy said prove it. Jean said im gonna tell you something and I need you to believe me after this a few days passed cindy and ryan was back home at work. Cindy got sick on her stomache took a pregnancy test and she was pregnant cindy yelled out o my god later that night she told ryan she was pregnant. Ryan was real happy he kissed her and said he loved her then ryan said whats wrong then cindy said I need to talk to you. He said ok what is it cindy said I see ghost ryan said and what that mean I still love you and we having a baby. And they hugged and kiss but no one knew what was gonna happen when the baby was born but cindy and jean. So they went on with they lives a few months later cindy went into labor and on the other side of town ryan was in a car accident. So cindy got to the hospital and the doctors told cindy her husband in the hospital too and cindy started to cry.

Friday, January 23, 20158:42 AM

CHAPTER 11

Turkey Terrorrated.r.

Back in 1985 in gainesville georgia in 1985 there was a family eating thanksgiving dinner when the turkey jumped up and cut the whole familys head off and then the turkey dissappeared. 15years passed and a family just moved to town there was 32year old Bob. wife 29 year old jane. And they 16year old son adam and they 8year old daughter jenny. They was a happy family one day Bob was at work and the kids was at school and jane was cleaning around the house when she heard a noise so she went to the kitchen where the noise was coming from but she saw nothing. So she went back to cleaning later that evening jane and the family was sitting down to dinner when they heard a glass brake Bob went to the kitchen and a glass had fell from the cabinet he said a glass fell from the cabinet and then he said I have to get someone to fix the cabinets. About 2am Bob went down to the kitchen to get some water and when he went in the kitchen there was a glass of water in the sank. Not thinking about it he drink the water. And went back to bed few days later jane was home alone and she heard a sound in the kitchen and she went to check it out. When she got to the kitchen the oven was on so she turned it off and went back to what she was doing later that night she

Things that Happened

told Bob that she needed to talk to him about something. Bob said what is it jane told Bob that earlier that day that she was cleaning the house and she heard a noise coming from the kitchen and when she got to the kitchen. The oven was on full force Bob said this is a old house and that the plugs was old and the cabinets he said sweetie you have a good imagination. Year later everyone in the neibor hood was getting turkeys and getting ready for thanksgiving coming soon 2am in the familys home jane could'nt sleep so she was reading a book when she heard a sound coming from down stairs. She went to see what it was because every body in the house was sleep. When jane got down stairs she went to the kinchen and she saw a figure standing by the stove then the figure turned around and looked at jane and said yall is gonna die then it dissappeared jane fainted the next morning Bob came down stairs and seen jane on the floor and he lift her up and said are you ok you need to go to the doctor jane said no im ok. Jane didn't tell Bob or the kids what she saw because she knod they would'nt believe her because she did'nt believe it her self a few days passed and jane heard a knock at the door and when she open the door there was her neibor trish. jane said come in and have some tea. And as the women sat drinking tea on the porch trish said how do you and your family like the house jane said its ok trish said just ok jane said its a house a roof over our heads. Trish said I need to tell you something but I don't know how you might re act. Jane said just tell me trish said it was a family lived here before yall but the family died all of them jane said you know I knew something was wrong trish said what do you mean jane said its nothing really trish said are you sure jane said yea im sure. Jane still can't believe what she saw and didn't want no one thinking she was crazy a few nights later jane and Bob was laying in bed and the kids was asleep in bed. Jane said Bob im gonna tell you something but I need to know that you are not gonna think im crazy Bob said tell me you know that you can tell me anything im not gonna think you crazy. Jane said one night a few months ago she could'nt sleep and she heard a noise and she went down stairs to the kitchen and she saw a figure of a person and it told her that they all was gonna die. Bob said what jane maybe you was sleep walking and dreaming she said I know what I saw then

# Butterfly Kisses

Bob said jane come here I do believe you then they started kissing and they made love. 2months later jane was getting dinner together and cleaning the turkey when she saw the figure again this time the figure told her don't be afraid im trying to worn you don't cook that turkey that her and her family lost they life because that turkey killed her and her family. Then it dissappeared. Then jane started thinking back when trish told her about the family got killed in this house. Then the turkey jumped up and said she was right now im gonna kill you and your family jane ran and was hollowing telling her family hurry we have to get out of here this house is haunted that the turkey trying to kill them. Bob said what are you saying then the turkey appeared and said she talking about me and then everyone ran out. but before they got out the turkey grabbed jane and Bob said please don't kill my wife and the turkey said yall been killing turkeys all yall humans life now its pay back. But janes son got behind the turkey and started stabbing him then he stabbed the turkey in the heart and killed him. 2years passed and the family was settled down in a new house and family and friends was coming over for thanksgiving and janes sister had a turkey jane. Stuck a knife in the turkeys heart and throwed it in the trash and went and joined her family then the garbbage can open the end. Story by Butterfly Kisses.

CHAPTER 12

The love he have for her

Back in 1998 there was 18 year old sandy now one night sandy was hanging out with her friend cathy at a party and sandy was introduce to 21 year old anthony. And sandy's friend cathy whisperd in sandy's ear and said have fun I will be back and both young women started laughing. Then anthony looked at sandy and said would you like for me to get you some punch sandy said you can but you don't have to try and get me drunk because I want you any way. Anthony looked at sandy and smiled and said for real and she said of course then he said what about your friend and sandy said she will be ok. Then sandy pulled anthony's arm and said come and they went to anthony's car where they made love. After it was over anthony took sandy home and sandy said I wont see you no more will I. anthony said yes you will, why you say that then sandy said because you got what you want right antHONY SAID NO I WAS GONNA GET TO KNOW YOU BETTER FIRST, YOU THE ONE WANTED TO DO THIS. SANDY SAID YOU RIGHT IM JUST BEING CRAZY AND AS SHE WAS GETTING OUT OF THE CAR ANTHONY SAID YOU NOT GETTING AWAY THAT EASY HE ASKED

 Butterfly Kisses

HER WHAT SHE WAS DOING THE NEXT night that he wanted to spend time TOGETHER I WANT TO GO TO THE MOVIES AND TAKE YOU TO DINNER SANDY SMILED WITH TEARS IN HER EYES AND KISSED HIM AND SAID SEE YOU TOMORROW NIGHT. IN YEAR 2000 SANDY AND ANTHONY HAD BEEN SEEING EACH OTHER FOR 2YEARS NOW IT WAS TIME FOR ANTHONY TO MEET THE PARENTS. HE WAS NERVOUS BUT IT HAD TO BE DONE ANTHONY ARRIVED AT sandy's PARENTS HOUSE AND SANDY'S DAD MARVE OPEN THE DOOR ANTHONY HAD LILY FLOWERS IN HIS HAND MARVE SAID YOU MUST BE ANTHONY AND HE SAID YES AND ANTHONY SAID YOU MUST BE MR WHITE AND MARVE SAID CALL ME MARVE. AND THEY SHOOK HANDS THEN MARVE SAID COME ON IN, THEN SANDYs, MOM AND SANDY WALKED UP AND SANDY'S MOM CAROLYN AND SANDY'S MOM SAID HELLO ANTHONY WEVE HEARD A LOT ABOUT YOU AND ANTHONY SAID ALL GOOD I HOPE. CAROLYN SAID ALL GOOD COME LETS SIT DOWN TO DINNER AS THEY WALKED TOWARD THE KITCHEN CAROLYN HUGGED SANDY AND SAID HE'S VERY NICE I LIKE. THEN THEY SIT DOWN TO DINNER WHEN MARVE STARTED ASKING ANTHONY ALL KIND of QUESTIONS AND THEN SANDY SAID DAD DON'T THEN MARVE SAID WHAT YOU KNOW HIM BUT WE DON'T. WE CAN ASK SOME QUESTIONS THEN ANTHONY said SIR I DON'T MEAN NO HOME BUT YOU QUESTION ME LIKE A CRIMINAL AND I DON'T LIKE it THEN HE LOOKED AT SANDY AND CAROLYN AND SAID IM SORRY BUT I HAVE TO GO. AND HE GOT UP AND LEF THEN SANDY SAID WHAT ARE YOU DOING AND CAROLYN SAID HE WAS A NICE MAN, YOU WAS WRONG MARVE. Then HE SAID DON'T YOU RUN AFTER HIM BECAUSE I WILL CUT YOU OUT OF OUR LIVES SANDY SAID IM GROWN DADDY GOODBYE. AND SHE SLAMMED THE DOOR AND LEF SANDY SAID

Things that Happened

ANTHONY PLEASE COME BACK ANTHONY YELLED NO IM SORRY AND HE PUllED OFF 3 MONTHS LATER. SANDY WAS WALKING IN TOWN SHOPPING WHEN SHE SEEN ANTHONY SHE said ANTHONY HEY AND HE SAID HEY, HEY, SANDY THEN A YOUNG WOMAN WALKED OUT AND SAID ANTHONY YOU READY. AND ANTHONY SAID SANDY THIS IS ROBERTA AND THE WOMEN SHAKED HANDS AND ANTHONY SAID SEE YOU SANDY AND SANDY SAID BYE. ALL THE REST OF THE DAY SANDY WAS UPSET BUT SHE HAD TO GO TO WORK SHE WORKED AT A LOCAL MOVIE THEATER. AND HER FRIEND THAT WORKED WITH HER NAME SHAN SAID SANDY ARE YOU OK SANDY SAID YES I WILL BE OK AND SHAN SAID YOU CANT LIE TO ME WHATS WRONG. SANDY SAID YOU REMEMBER THE GUY I TOLD YOU ABOUT MY DAD RAN OFF SHAN SAID YES SANDY SAID I SEEN HIM TODAY AND SHAN SAID WHAT HAPPEN AND SANDY SAID HE WAS WITH A WOMAN. SHAN SAID WHAT AND SANDY SAID YES THEN SHAN SAID WELL THAT'S HIS LOST BECAUSE YOU ARE BEATIFUL MY GIRL AND SANDY STARTED SMILING AND SAID THATS RIGHT GIRL AND THEY HIT HANDS AND STARTED LAUGHING. 4YEARS PASSED AND SANDY WAS 24YEARS OLD ONE NIGHT SANDY AND SHAN WAS AT A NIGHT CLUB AND THIS BIG MAN CAME UP TO SANDY AND SAID HEY BABY. HOW ARE YOU AND SANDY SAID IM GOOD AND THE MAN NAME WAS RAY AND HE SAID WOULD YOU LADIES LIKE TO HANG OUT WITH ME AND MY FRIEND AND HE CALLED THE MAN WHO WORK WITH HIM. WHO NAME WAS JAMES AND SHAN SAID YOU BET YOUR BUT WE WILL AND THEY LEF WITH THE GUYS LATER THAT NIGHT RAY LOOKED AT SANDY AND SAID DO YOU KNOW A GUY NAME ANTHONY AND SANDY SAID YES BUT HE'S A JERK THE MAN BUST OUT LAUGHING AND SANDY SAID Well HE IS A JERK THEN RAY SAID

 Butterfly Kisses

I WORK FOR ANTHONY AND SANDY SAID WHAT DO YOU MEAN AND RAY SAID HE'S MY BOSS. SANDY SAID GET OUT OF HERE IM LEAVING AS SHE WAS WALKING AWAY RAY HIT HER IN THE BACK OF HER HEAD AND SHE PASSED OUT.

SHE WOKE UP THE NEXT MORNING IN A LOCKED ROOM AND THERE WAS ANTHONY AND SaNDY SAID WHAT ARE YOU DOING ANTHONY AND HE SAID I GOT YOU HELD HOSTAGE TO DEAR OLD DADDY COME AND GET YOU THEN SANDY SAID YOU KNOW I DIDN'T HAVE NOTHING. TO DO WITH IT AND ANTHONY SAID I KNOW BUT YOUR DAD WILL COME AND IM GONNA KILL HIM SANDY STARTED SCREAMING SAYING NO PLEASE ANTHONY NO THEN ANTHONY KISSED HER ON HER FORE HEAD AND SAID YES. LATER THAT NIGHT MARVE SHOWED UP AND SANDY OVER HEARD THEM TALKING AND SANDY HEARD HER DAD SAY WE DEALERS I CANT LET YOU DATE MY DAUGHTER. THEN ANTHONY OPEN THE DOOR WHERE SANDY WAS AND SHE SAID DAD HOW COULD YOU THEN SHE JUMPED UP And SAID YOU WILL NEVER SEE ME AGAIN. THEN MARVE SAID WHAT HAVE YOU DONE BY THIS TIME SHAN WAS CALLING THE POLICE AND MARVE PULLED A GUN AND SHOT ANTHONY AND SANDY LOOKED AT HER DAD AND SAID YOU GOING TO JAIL AND THEN MARVE TRIED TO SHOOT SANDY AND SHAN GOT A GUN AND SHOT HIM THEN THE POLICE GOT THERE AND MARVE WENT TO THE HOSPITAL FEW DAYS LATER A JURY FOUND HIM GUITY AND SENT HIM TO PRISON FOR 65YEARS WITHOUT PAROLE. NOW SANDY AND HER MOM SPEND A LOT OF TIME TOGETHER SANDY STILL HAVE HER JOB AND HER AND SHAN STILL FRIENDS AND THEY WAS AT A PARTY AND A CUTE GUY TRIED TO TALK TO HER BUT SANDY SAID NO THANKS AND SHAN GRABBED HER ARM AND THEY LEF THE END. LET ME INTRODUCE MY SELF IM BUTTERFLY KISSESAND I WROTE THIS STORY HOPE

Things that Happened

MY READERS IN JOY BUT FIRST I HAVE TO THANK GOD AND OUR LORD SAVIOR JESUS CHRIST IF IT WASN'T FOR MY LORD, GOD I Wound'nt BE WRITING THESE STORY'S ALL THAnks TO GOD, THANKYOU JESUS PRAISE GOD EVERYONE BE BLESSED.

Friday, A-pril 17, 20151:43 PM

CHAPTER 13

Crew

Back in year 1975 there was a young man name que now this young man was very queit hung out by him self everytime you saw him he was walking and hanging out by him self. Until one night he was passing by this club called big fred's night shack and que always wonderd what all happen in that club. This night the owner of the club big fred him self walked out of the door and said whats going on young man. whats your name and he said que my name is que and then the big man said hey que my name is big fred. Then they both shook hands then big fred said would you like to come in and que said I don't know then big fred said its ok come on in. Then que said alright just for a minutes but when que came in he liked it so much he stayed til morning. 23years passed and que grew up so que and his best friend went to the beach to find some girls and when they arrived at the beach there was a lot of girls believe it or not. But que didn't see no one he wanted so he and friend jason lef that night que was at home alone and he was laying on his bed when all of a sudden his stomache started hurting and he started hollowing real loud in a deep voice and then. Que jumped out of his window, one month later que was driving around and he saw a

Things that Happened

young woman walking the streets and he pulled his car over on the side of the road and ask the young woman did she need a ride. And the young woman her name was jess said sure and que said where are you going and jess said home please. Then they was riding in que's car when jess said you passed my street and then que started driving faster and went down this side street and hit jess hard in her face and she passed out. Next thing que was eating her like she was food and then he buried her in a shadow grave a few months passed and que and his friend was back at the beach. And this time que saw a woman laying on a beach tower with a bikini and shades on her eyes and que walked up to her and said hello beautiful. How are you and she looked up at him and said im fine how are you then que said im a lot better since I seen you and she smiled and said im aime and do you say this to every woman you meet be honest. And then que said I have to think and then he said no then que said do you have a man I know you do fine is you is. Aime said no not now then que said do you have a number aime said sure I do what about you and que yelled out his number and then aime told que her number. Then aime said I have to go I will call you and then aime said you call me too and she walked away in slow motion as que watched her from head to toe. A coupler nights later que picked up another woman and dumped her body and then his phone rung and it was aime and she said hey que whats going on and que said nothing at home im relaxing tonight then aime said. Well I guess you to tied to see me and then que thought to him self I can see her because I already fed and then que said where are you and aime said. At my house on carolina street and he said you just right around the corner from me be therein five be ready and she smiled and said you bet I will be ready. So que went to pick up aime and she had on this long over coat and long legs and black heels on that tie around her ankles. Then she got into que's car and they went to que's house and aime said you have a big house and its beautiful and you stay here alone and que said yes and aime said its beautiful and. Que said not as beautiful as you are then aime open her coat and she had only pantis and bra on and que walked up to her and they started kissing and they made love right there on the floor. The next morning aime woke up and que was exerciseing

and she layed there and looked at him then she smiled and said good morning and que said good morning I fixed breakfast are you hungry and aime said starving and she put on a house coat and said let's eat. And from that day forward que and aime started seeing each other but some times aime wonderd why some times she wouldn't see que for a few days. And one evening aime called que's phone and que answerd the phone but he talked like he was mad about something and then aime said whats the matter and que said aime you just call and call all day long and aime said I love you and que said see that's what im talking about. Aime said I see you upset about something I will talk to you later but please tell me you not seeing no one else que said no im not you the only one in my life. Then aime said ok i'll talk to you later then she hung up the phone few days later aime was at home eating pop corn sitting watching a movie. Then there was a knock at the door aime went to the door and said who is it then que said me and aime yelled through the door what do you want, que said amie open the door im here to see you and aime said so now you want to see me and que said you know I do. Then que said aime im sorry what else can I say please open the door let me explain then aime open the door and said. Whats going on and que said can we sit down and then que started crying and said aime I need to tell you something and, I don't know how to tell you this because im so in love with you, aime said que you can tell me anything and im still gonna love you. Then que said come sit next to me and aime did she said what is it you scaring me then que said when I was younger. I went in this club one night called big fred's and I really cant explain what happen but I woke up the next morning and when I got grown things started happenimg that I cant explain and I

cant control it. Aime said what are you telling me que are you killing people as she reached in her draw and pulled out her small gun and she quickley pulled the safety off her gun and pointed it at him. And aime said answer me are you killing people then que dropped his head and said not killing them but eating them. Then aime said why other people but not me then que said because I cant hurt what I love I made a promise to my self not to hurt no one I love. Then aime said I think you need to leave here and never come back. And

Things that Happened

then she yelled and said get out get out I don't never want to see you again then que cried and said im so sorry aime I didn't know I was ever gonna fall in love. And then he lef for the next few days aime was sitting at home thinking about what all que said and she had tears in her eye, s and she didn't know what to do. So aime went to see a lady in they town called madam ann and she told madam ann what was happening and ann was kind of afraid but she asked aime did she love this man and aime said more than you know then, aime said can you help him and aime had tears in her eyes I know he love me because he never hurt me and he could have, but he didn't. Then madam ann said I can give you something to help him but you will bring out whats in him are you ready aime said yes. Then madam ann gave aime a little small grey bag and said you have to put this in his dinner and then madam ann said please becareful and madam ann said you not gonna like what you see come out but you will save your love. Then aime hugged madam ann and said thank you then she lef two days later aime called que and said im sorry that I act like I did do you forgive me and que said yes then aime said ive made dinner come over. And que said ok but aint you scared of me aime said no should I bee she said I don't think you will hurt me because you love me right, que said yes I do then que said I will be there in ten minutes. Aime said I will be waiting, 20 minutes later que arrived and aime open the door and hugged and kissed him and then they sat down to eat when. Everything was going good at first and then que fell to the floor and started yelling loud and then aime ran out the door. And aime still heard que yelling and after a few minutes everything got real quiet and aime ran into the house where she saw a big large creature standing over que and then the large monster looked at aime and said I will be back and the monster disappeared. Then aime grabbed que and said you are free and que hugged aime back and said thankyou, and aime said you welcome. A month later aime and que walked by madam ann and she came out side and said I see everything worked out. And aime said yes it did thankyou and aime and que walked off and madam ann looked at them and smiled but then she got a feeling in her stomache because she knew that the monster was coming back one day and she dropped her head the

 Butterfly Kisses

end. Allow me to introduce my self my name is Butterfly Kisses and I just wrote this story and I hope everyone enjoy it because my book is for everyone to read hope yall enjoy. You know if it wasn't for my heavenly father in heaven my lord, god I wouldn't be able to write my stories I give all the credit to my heavenly father me and husband Bob believe in our lord, god very much and always will no matter what so thankyou all and may god, bless everyone.

Saturday, April 18, 2015 2:49 PM

CHAPTER 14

The Good Twin and the Bad Twin

In the town of dallas texas there was 22 year old tea and 22 year old twin sister lea now as you know sometimes twins could be good or bad and one of these twins was very good and the other was very bad. Tea was good everyone liked her but everyone was very afraid of her twin sister lea because when people would see lea she always looked. mean at people so no one in town ever spoke to lea now one night tea was asked to a party and she SAID YES I WILL GO WITH YOU SO TEA AND FRIEND WENT TO THE PARTY AND WAS HAVING A GOOD TIME. BUT WHEN TEA GOT HOME HER SISTER WAS WAITING FOR HER LEA LOOKED AT TEA AND SAID YOU ARE NO DIFFRIENT THAN I AM. AND TEA SAID GOOD NIGHT LEA ONE MONTH PASSED AND TEA STARTED DATING HER FRIEND JACOB. AND ONE NIGHT JACOB AND TEA WAS HAVING DINNER AND JACOB ASKED TEA TO MOVE IN WITH HIM HE SAID HE WAS FALLING FOR HER REAL HARD. THEN TEA SAID THAT SHE WOULD BUT THAT SHE HAD TO LET LEA KNOW

Butterfly Kisses

AND JACOB SAID OK AND TEA DID TELL HER SISTER. TEA SAID IM STILL GONNA BE OVER HERE EVERYDAY TO SEE MY SISTER. THEN LEA SAID YOU DON'T HAVE TO DO THAT IM A BIG GIRL AND LEA WALKED OUT OF THE ROOM THEN TEA PHONE RING AND IT WAS JACOB HE SAID DO YOU NEED ME TO COME AND GET YOU AND YOUR STUFF. AND TEA SAID YES WOULD YOU AND

JACOB SAID IM ON MY WAY 15 MINUTES LATER JACOB DROVE UP AND ALL THIS TIME LEA WAS STANDING IN A BEDROOM WINDOW LOOKING AT TEA AND JACOB. THEN TEA HOLLOWED AND SAID IM GONE LEA YOU AINT GONNA COME AND SEE ME OFF LEA SAID GOODBYE SISTER FOR NOW BECause you will be back. And lea looked at jacob real hard and said because jacob is gay then tea told jacob gone to the car she would be there shortly. Jacob said ok then tea looked at lea and said I know why you so alone because you are so mean to people and that's ugly. You need to leave jacob alone because I love him and one day he will be my husband do you understand goodbye lea I do hope that you be happy here alone. And tea went out the and lea was standing there in a naked jay and jacob dropped everything and went and made love to lea. Later that night lea sneaked out of the house and tea came home and got in the bed. And jacob said hey baby where did you go it was like he was talking in his sleep so tea didn't say anything. One month later lea was up to her old tricks she thought that tea was gonna be on call so she went over and got in the bed with jacob. And tea came home and went in the house and opened the door and slammed it. few months later tea took a job that caused her to work longer hours she had went to college to become a doctor so. She was at the hospital on call a lot why jacob was at home one night lea went to tea and jacob's house jacob was in the bed asleep. And lea went in the bed room like she was tea and jacob didn't know it was lea he thought it was tea and he had sex with lea. The next morning tea was down stairs making breakfast and jacob woke up happy and he thanked tea but she thought he was talking about her making breakfast. So tea said you welcome and jacob grabbed breakfast and kissed tea and said he loved her and he would see her this evening. And tea said I will be here because I suppose to be off and jacob smiled and said ok and he lef later that day tea got a call from the hospital that she was needed. And she tried to call jacob but did not reach him so she went to work all this time lea was watching and listening to everything so she was at tea and jacob's house again. As you know jacob don't know that this is lea he think that lea is tea so jacob got home nothing without our lord, god everyone out there be blessed put your trust in lord jesus lord god.

Monday, April 20, 2015 9:15 PM

CHAPTER 15

The Story of All People

In our lord, god's world and on his earth and me my self ive had one best friend keisha brewton she's dead now. And ive had a older lady friend I still see her every once and a while well what im trying to say is that I don't really be around a lot of people because I don't really like no crowd when I was seven I was raped and I think. It took a whole part of me I don't know if its that I cant believe that it happen but it did and I cant. Shake it off but you know with the love my lord, god have for me that keep me going. My lord, god, gives me lot's of things to keep me going every day my lord blessed me with my family to surround me each and every day my loving husband Bob he supports me. When I need to get it off my chest and when I need a shoulder to cry on because believe or not ive been through some things since I been grown. I iknow a little about being jumped on when I was going to school I had girls that ganged me and I also had cousins to help to get them off my back. Me and husband lost our baby's that was our first together but we know our babies is with our lord, god me and husband and I have cousins as well that do believe in the living lord, god, in heaven. You know there is a lot of people out here in the world that is being beated rather its by a boyfreind are a husband, wife, and its a lot of people that's afraid to tell anyone. They so afraid they want even tell they parents and no one knows until something bad happen like some one is dead. And you know that's bad its real bad That's stuff people go through also its people in the world that is bruising children and taking them off raping and killing our children. Some times it be people you know are you think you know them and its people trying to get pregnant and can't but some people can have babies back to back some cant. And I mean these people love kids just can't have kids you know me and husband had a etopic pregnancy and I lost one of my tubes I have another one but its damaged. And doctor said we want have no more kids I always say to my husband that my doctor is not god and I know this I believe in my heavenly father in heaven so much I know that if we mint to get pregnant again we will. I only believe in my lord, god always well I have a 27year old son that's married and very happy and kids and grand kids also my husband have a 18year old son dontaye j. And we say that both are our children we love them so much well let me continue my story you know how people say that your family is the ones that talk about you well I know a lot of people that do this and its not good that causes a lot of problems. You know I didn't think I would see so much going on some my family and some others family you know stuff like this break up familys. And that's really not good because god made all of us and our lord, god don't treat us no diffrient he want all us to love one another. Some do and some don't also there people out here killing each other our young people is killing they own and they act like they don't care and that's bad. But you know its not really the world its the people in it and also a lot of people walk around here having diffrient thoughts that they don't need no one but thats not true at all we always need some one or something and I know we all need god for the. rest of our lives I tell you another thing we people out here talking about our homeless when every one need to be helping them instead of putting our head up in cloud nine you know me and husband talk about this a lot how this could be us. Im just telling the truth im gonna be very honest to my readers and maybe one day my fans me and husband use to steal lights. Like I said may I tell the truth I use to be a big drinker

 Butterfly Kisses

its just so much I see in the world it will blow your mine when me and husand Bob went to charlotte we helped homeless people me and Bob have homeless people in our town. That it will make your head spend that's how bad it is if I can help people I will but im the type of person im not gonna be no fool. For no one not long as I can help it now let me talk a little bit about people and church now my husband joined the church september 22 2013 and I join another church cornerstone baptist church. Bob got baptize on his moms birthday now that was special and me and mother inlaw betty we was at the church when he was baptized it was a great day. Every day is a great day when we wake up because we don't wake our selves up our lord, god wake us up and things would be a lot better if anough of us believed by knowing the lord, god real and not by seeing what else can I say now. I cant make nobody believe but I can put it out there if there is someone out there that don't know the lord, god its not to late. When I was real young people use to come and talk to me about the lord, god and I use to go the other way but today and every day. I cant wait to go to church and learn more and more because I do believe and always will no matter what as I said I do believe in god I have my daddy's mother mrs wilma jean burpo. And if lord's willing in june 2015 she will be 80years old now you tell me god's not real and very good. My grand ma gets around better then I do and all her kids is alive accept my one uncle my mom been dead going on a year so now my grand ma is my big mom and dad james brannon is still alive thank our lord jesus, lord god. Well this is the end of this story but everyone take care of each other and love everyone I know that its hard but our lord, god said in the bible revenge is his not ours well I hope that every one enjoy reading my short stories my name is Butterfly Kisses and I wrote this story. Will be back real soon everyone be blessed.

    Tuesday, April 21, 2015 4:06 PM

CHAPTER 16

The Long Love

My story starts out with janice and husband micheal now these to people dated on and off ad never ever thought they would ever get married. Well let me start from the beginning janice dated micheal back when they was younger but something happen that the two had got split up. But micheal came back looking for janice and she was gone and she didn't have no phone to be reach so micheal. Went back to where he had to go in the first place which was the service and janice went on with her life. Every one that janice tried to date would not be micheal. During this time janice was sent down to a girls home. Because she wouldn't go to school back in 1987 janice became pregnant and in the year 1988 janice gave birth to a son she name peter. Now janice had to give all her time to her son so janise didn't go out and she didn't want peters father so she was on her on she always had her lord, god and her mom. One day janice met some one and after a while she married this man but she really wasn't in love with him but she stayed with him until he died and she became a widow. Janice was still young the husband was older so after he died she didn't know what a widow was to do so she started going out and partying. Drinking everyday she had became a big drunk and doing

 Butterfly Kisses

drugs and sleeping around but after a while she met another older man that ran a liquor house. And he would buy janice her own drink he kept her with cigerettes anything she needed money some times and she smoked her drugs. Janice was out in the world bad and she also was staying with another man at the time she was seeing this older man. He was married but she went with him any way after a while janice had her own liquor house she still was drinking but not that much she was making a lot of money. Janice had this house for a long time until this older man that was saling liquor from his car got jealous and threating to tell the police on her. So janice had to close up her house and move when janice got moved she had a birthday party and every body came. And even her old boyfriend micheal was there janice could not believe it she told her older friend lady that she use to date that guy and she pointed at micheal. But guess what when micheal was young he was skinny but now he was big and tall janice singed some songs for her guess and micheal could not believe it when micheal got ready to leave he pulled janice a side and said give him a kiss if she scared say she scared. And janice gave him a big kiss after that night one month later janice ran into micheal and this time she got his number and 3rd time she saw him they started dating. And micheal started taking care of her and they moved with his mom and then they got they own place then janice got pregnant by micheal and. And they baby died after that janice said no more babies and sure enough her doctor said she couldn't have no more children but janice had a grown son and micheal had a child they both living thank god well janice and micheal still was together taking they time. To get married so a time came around when janice and micheal got a cousin to plan they wedding and janice said it was worth the wait it took three months to get everything done for the wedding but it went great. Janice daddy walked her down to the alter it was beautiful after janice and micheal was married they went on a great honey moon and then they went to the queen city it was very nice. Time they got married they rode in a rose royce it was very neat now the couple done been married for almost 2 months they still newly weds and how about when the two first met back up. They didn't have but. one picture together now they got a whole lot and more and thanks to the lord, god the couple believe in the lord jesus christ the lord god always because janice and micheal know that our heavenly father get all credit because they know that our lord, god put them back together. And this was his will and everyone should give all glory to god praise his name hallilua thank you jesus well the couple to day which is 2015 they doing very good thank god well this is the end of my story true story my name is Butterfly Kisses and I just wrote this true tale well accept christ as yall lord we cant do this by our self we all need our lord, god well everyone out there god bless you all.

Saturday, April 18, 2015 3:27 PM

CHAPTER 17

The Lonely One

Here is 30 year old simon now he was a very neat person everything in simons house was put very neatly and if he had company like friends come over. After they lef he would clean behind them especially if some one used his bath room he scrubbed everything he was what we would call a neat freak. One evening simon went out to a bar where he met 28 year old sara they sat at the bar drinked and laughed and talk and had a great time. Then simon told sara that he was strange and sara said what do you mean and simon said a lot of people call me weird still sara said I don't know what u mean. Simon said im a neat freak and sara said really how neat are you and simone said if you see my house you would say nobody live there. Then sara said wild Then simon said now you think im weird right, sara said no not really as long as you don't think you better then me simon said I will never think that. But we might have some problems because I would need for you to help keep the place nice clean and neat. Sara said I will but im not a maid or robot simon said that's all I ask im not calling you a maid or nothing like that. Then they started dating but sara didn't move in right away because she wanted to see how things go between her and simon. Everything seemed great and sara

Things that Happened

even spent the night with simon. But one morning sara had fixed breakfast and the kitchen was a mess simon came down stairs and when he saw the kitchen he freaked out and told sara she had to go. Then sara said whats wrong simon and he said look at this mess you made a big mess in my kitchen just leave. Sara lef and she was very upset because she knew something would happen that's why she didn't move in with him. But she went on with her life 2monthes later sara met some one else 29year old tate and tate treated sara very good and sara fell for tate right away and the two moved in with one another. One night tate had cooked dinner for sara and she was real happy and then tate got on his knees and said sara will you marry me and sara had tears in her eyes and said yes I will marry you. A few months passed and sara was out shopping when she ran into guess who simon and simon said how are you and sara said im good how about you. Simon said im great now that I see you. And sara said, o, what do you mean and simon said I want you back and sara said well you to late im ingaged and im very happy then simon said well that's good then sara said I have to go it was good to see you but my fiance who I love is waiting for me goodbye. When sara got home and told tate that she just seen simon at the store and tate said what happen and sara said nothing I said hey and I came home to the man I love and tate grabbed her and hugged her. 2months later sara and tate got married went on they honeymoon where they had a great time sara didn't want to leave. All during this time simon was following sara and tate after the honeymoon the two got home back to work and one evening sara was making a special dinner for her and tate. When there was a knock at the door guess who it was it was simon and sara said simon why are you here simon pulled out a gun and said get in the house. Then sara said what you gonna do kill me, simon said yes but not before I kill your perfect husband simon said I followed yall and you was having fun on your honeymoon sara said simon do what you gonna do and leave and simon said I have to wait for your hubby. Then sara said simon what do you want and simon said I cant have you and tate not either then sara said how do you know his name and simon said we all growed up together. I aint never liked him he always thought he was better then us then tate was rattling

keys and simon hid and tate came in saying hey honey how was your day. And then he saw sara tied up and tape on her mouth and then simon walked up behind tate and hit him in the head and sara was screaming. And they next door neibor heard the noise and called the police by this time tate saw a way to jump across the room and he did he jumped on top of tate and the gun slid across the floor and sara got it but there was no bullets in the gun and then simon went toward sara when a shot came through the side door and hit simon. The police got there and saw what was happening and the police said yall neibor called 911 and we came right away he asked was they ok and they said thanks to you we good thank you and simon lived and the jury found him guity of all counts and the judge gave him life. 1year later sara and tate had a cook out and all they family and friends was there then sara looked at tate and said I love you more and more everyday and then tate said I love you very much and they kissed the end also sara and tate in church they have two kids and they all thank god every day because they know god saved them not the cop god sent the police there just in time to save they life. The end. Allow me to introduce my self im Butterfly Kisses and im from spartanburg sc born and raised and im happily married to husband Bob and we have a big family that we love very much but first of all we love our lord and savior jesus christ our lord god well this is the end, this is the end of my first book I hope that yall enjoy it thank you all and god bless all.

Wednesday, April 22, 2015 5:40 PM

CHAPTER 18

All the Children in the World

My story begin by talking about african american kids american white kids indian kids chinese kids and our mixed kids and grand kids and great grand kids. This story talks about how all our children in the world is not different no matter what color we are god love all because they all come from god. I sit back and watch a lot of stuff all different colors are against one another because the color of our skin. And that's bad we all should get alone even if we don't want to because we cant judge one another because only god judge us all we all sit around and love whats ours and we should but in. gods eyes we all are brothers and sisters moms dads grand parents aunts uncles all kind of kin and we really fail to realize that, and in the middle of all this there are our children some try to get alone but some grow up hating one another if they aint fighting against one another they killing one another are killing same colors its not good and us as parents sit back and let it happen me and husband Bob we have a 18 year old son and a 28 year old and im not saying they perfect because the only one perfect is our lord jesus christ. But we can say that we do a good job with them with the help of our lord, god another thing we have other kids picking

 Butterfly Kisses

at our mix kids they still is part of all of us no matter what. All the kids in the world belong to every one in gods eyes taking from me im a full african american woman and when I went to school I had kids that picked fights with me all the time I mean gangs of kids. unto one day I got tired and fighted back but this styory is about all the kids in the world no matter who they is. Rather they are our kids or other people kids and for our parents that work I know you have to work but the first day you be off spend it with your kids even if its to make them ice cream cones in the house watching a family movie. Just do something because some kids growing up saying what they parents didn't do for them and how they barely saw parents when they growed up. But kids parents do have to work to take care of all our children but then theres parents out here beat they kids im not talking about a whooping im talking about abusing them and there are some step parents abusing our kids like. Sexual abuse and some out side people that's abusing them and people doing just to be doing and that make kids grow up with so much hate in they heart they either abuse they spouse or they children and robbing and killing one another and taking whats not theres they steal take stuff that's not theres and its not right but it happens. Because that's the way they was brought up and then us parents wonder what happen but we never think about what that child be done went through that's we as parents we need to sit back and just watch different stuff that our children do and things they say. Some parents might say that child is just trying to get attention in some ways that might be true but in other words it might not be true. Im not trying to tell no one what to do im just saying we need to listen to our kids a lot more then what we do because the late mrs whidney houston said it right the children are our future what they learn from us can either help them in the future with they kids or not. Its just a chance we have to take, so this story is all about our children and they future. kids are the beautifuls things on our lord, gods earth so please keep in mind that our kids are our future don't forget it the end. Allow me to introduce myself im Butterfly Kisses and my writing is a gift from our lord, god and I thank god every day for my talent and I really love our lord, god forever and ever may all be blessed.

Wednesday, April 29, 2015 11:52 AM

CHAPTER 19

Title the Children Story

April 29.2015 4.09pm

There was 8 year old peter and this little boy had a very good imagination every toy in his room he always would say they was alive but his dad always would say yea, yea,. So one day peter was out at the mall with his dad jake, and peter and his dad passed this children store and peter said dad please lets go in this store. And jake said ok and they went in the store and peter saw a toy that sat by it self but the toy was kind of high at the price but peter wanted this toy and he told his dad I will work for this toy. And jake said ok but you will have to do a lot around the house before I give him to you peter said thanks dad thanks. So people did all his chores around the house to get his new toy one evening peters dad was going out with some friends. And peter had a baby sitter peter kissed his dad and said goodnight dad and his dad said goodnight peter. And his dad lef peter told his baby sitter cher that he was going to his room to play with his toys and then go to bed. Then cher said don't forget to brush your teeth and he said yes mam and he went to his room

and peter closed his door and pulled out his new toy. And guess what happen his new toy was a robot and it was alive peter said you really is alive and his robot said yes and I can help all children and peter said wow. Then it was time for peter to go to bed he brushed his teeth and said his prayers and layed down with his new friend. A few hours later peter was sleep and his robot friend heard a scream like some one was in trouble so his robot growed a little big and went out the window and saved this lady's life and he looked at the lady and said don't tell no one about me im a hero and my name is hal and im here to protect all, especially kids. The next morning peter was eating breakfast and his dad was reading the news paper and he said peter we have a new hero in town and peter said what do you mean dad and jake said in the news paper a homeless lady got saved by what she call her guardian angel. Peter said wow then peter had to go to school and when he got out of school he done his home work and ate dinner and played with his new friend. Then peter said I know your name its hal and his robot said how do you know and peter said you helped that lady last night. And hal said yes I did and peter said that's cool then hal said how would you like to help me, and peter said yes I will help but I would need a costume and hal made a suit appear and peter said you can do magic and hal said yes I can. Later that night hal told people its time, that this time it was a little girl they had to save so they went to the little girls house and the little girl let them in the window then the little girl looked at hal and peter. And said wow, cool who are yall and they told her they was heros here to save all kids. and she told the heros that she was afraid of the dark and hal made a special little doll appear and gave it to the little girl and said when you get scared hug your doll and you will feel safe. And from that night on peter was helping hal they went every where happen kids and kids loved them into one day peter fail a sleep in class and the school called peter's dad jake and told him and at dinner jake said is there. something You need to talk about and peter said no sir and his dad said the school called and peter said dad I need to tell you something and jake said what is it. And peter said you know all the kids who was save by what they call a hero jake said yes what about it peter said hal did it jake said who is hal and peter said my robot

Things that Happened

jake said what, what are you talking about your robot helped saved kids peter said yes sir and jake said yea right peter go to your room and peter said dad and his dad said go ahead now. And peter told hal that his dad didn't belive him and hal said if I show your dad that im alive then I really wont be alive ever again because that's a rule where im from. Then hal said im gonna do it because you my best friend and I love you peter. Then hal growed a little and went down stairs and said. See peter wasn't lying im real and I saved them kids me and with the help of peter you should be proud of him. Then jake took off his glasses and said im dreaming and then hal touched jake and said no you not dreaming and then jake called peter and said come here. And peter said dad I told you he was alive and from that night on peter helped hal keep kids safe and jake said peter I love you and I always will no matter what and he kissed peter on his fore head and then kissed hal on his fore head and said I love you too hal and the robot smiled the end. Allow me to introduce my self im Butterfly Kisses and I just wrote this children story my first children story and I couldn't do it with out our lord, god and im gonna always thank my lord, god in heaven well I hope everyone enjoy my story's may all be blessed I will like to thank my husband Bob for supporting me in my books as well all be bless.

Wednesday, April 29, 2015 1:07 PM

CHAPTER 20

The Writer

April. 29th 2015, time, 11.39 am.

This story starts out with 40 year old kurt rodgers he was a writer of all different kinds of story's he wrote romance's horror's drama's and christian storys. One day kurt sat down with his cup of coffee and a dozen of donuts and he just started writing. And his story was about a writer who worked all the time and barely had time to date so he decided that he was gonna take a break from writing and try and meet the right woman. He had his eyes on 39 year old nicole jazz but she knew that kurt enjoyed his work that it kept him going. And at first she didn't want to go out with him but one Friday night she went to have dinner with kurt just as friends but it turned out very different she really wanted to get to know kurt a lot better. One night kurt invited nicole over for some wine and dinner and nicole arrived and her and kurt was sitting down talking and nicole said kurt I realy do like you. But I also know by you being a writer that some times I wont see you and kurt dropped his head and said that's true. And then kurt said what are we gonna do about it and then nicole went and sat down beside kurt. And said I don't know and then they started to kiss and made love right there on the couch and the next morning. When nicole woke up she went into the kitchen and there was breakfast and then kurt came in from his office and kissed her and said good morning and nicole said good morning where was you. He said just finishing up something and nicole said im gonna get dress and I have somethings to finish up my self. Then kurt said ok well I guess I will see you later and nicole said ok if im not to busy are don't have nothing to do. Kurt said I understand and nicole lef after that kurt was so busy writing til he never relized that he have.nt seen nicolle in a while so that night he went by nicole's house. And he ring the door bell and nicole came to the door and said well look who it is and she had been drinking. Then kurt said im so sorry and nicole said that's alwright I know that by you being a writer you have to give that all your attention. Then kurt said no its not like that at all and then nicole said well what is it and kurt said I cant explain but im not gonna lie to you. Then nicole said kurt come in and sit down and she asked him did he want something to drink and he said yes I would like you very wet and nicole said no kurt not none of that im just seeing you after a month. Then kurt got up and hugged nicole and she hugged him back as tears was running down her face and kurt said im so so sorry please forgive me and kurt said what can I do to make things better between us. And nicole said kurt I understand that you're a writer and that's your work but nicole said in order for our relationship to go any further we need to spend a little more time together and then you can go back to your work. when kurt got down on one knee and pulled out a beautiful diamond ring and said nicole will you marry me. And nicole said with tears in her eyes I will marry you but you have to promise that you will spend a little more time with me too. And kurt said I do promise as he put the ring on her finger and they kissed and made love 2months later kurt married nicole in front of friends and family. 1 year passed and and it was back the work for kurt one day nicole came in with some grocerys and she said hey honey im home. But there was no answer so nicole went to kurts office and kurt was in there writing and nicole said kurt I know you back at writing but when I get home

 Butterfly Kisses

you can say hey or something. And she walked out of the room kurt ran behind her and grabbed her arm and said you knew what I did before we married and kurt said I never said that it was gonna be easy. Then nicole said that's true but one day its gonna be me or your work and she walked off as kurt stood there and looked at her. One month later kurt cooked dinner and lit candles and put out some of nicoles favorite wine and he dressed nice and also kurt called his publisher and told him that he wrote the books and what he said goes and kurts publisher tony said ok. Whats this about kurt said im just writing and aint spent no time with my wife he said I will be in touch. And hung up the phone and then 5minutes later tony called and said I have some good news. And kurt said what is it and tony said. After this book you just wrote it sold millions so you don't have to write for 2 years then kurt yelled yes thankyou and tony said you welcome congraulations and tony said kurt say hello to nicole and tell her thankyou for putting up with us. Later nicole came home and said kurt whats going on and kurt told nicole the good news and they hugged and kissed and nicole said im pregnant and kurt picked her up and said I love you and nicole said I love you to the end. my name is Butterfly Kisses and I just wrote this story and I cound not have done this without my heavenly father jesus christ and my lord god I give all credit to my lord, god always and me and husband Bob do to, well until next story thank you and may god bless all.

Tuesday, April 28, 2015 11:41 AM

www.ingramcontent.com/pod-product-compliance
Ingram Content Group UK Ltd.
Pitfield, Milton Keynes, MK11 3LW, UK
UKHW041956230426
12048UKWH00008B/374